To my mother, who loves children and children's books.

—B.L.

For our friends Joe and Naomi Richard
and their cat family: Bodger, Chicken, and Clara.
And for our friends Bill and Marsha Dehn
and their cat family: Hadley, Fleur, and Travis.
This is a mostly true story about one of the above-mentioned
cats—only the name has been changed to spare "Furlie" embarrassment.

—B.F.

This book is a presentation of Weekly Reader Books.
Weekly Reader Books offers book clubs for children from preschool through high school.
For further information write to:
Weekly Reader Books, 4343 Equity Drive, Columbus, Ohio 43228.

Published by arrangement with Lothrop, Lee & Shepard Books.

First Edition 1 2 3 4 5 6 7 8 9 10

Library of Congress Cataloging in Publication Data Freschet, Berniece. Furlie cat. Summary: Afraid of almost everything, Furlie Cat becomes a bully scaring everyone else until the night he is trapped in a tree. [1. Cats—Fiction. 2. Fear—Fiction. 3. Bullies—Fiction] I. Lewin, Betsy, ill. II. Title. PZ7.F88968Fu 1986 [E] 85-11656
ISBN 0-688-05917-1 ISBN 0-688-05918-X (lib. bdg.)

Weekly Reader Children's Book Club presents

by Berniece Freschet

Pictures by Betsy Lewin

LOTHROP, LEE & SHEPARD BOOKS
NEW YORK

Furlie Cat lived in an old brown house with a crooked climbing tree in front. Except for one white eye patch, and two white front paws, Furlie's fur was orange.

The tip of Furlie's right ear bent forward, giving him the look of a tough little cat who liked to fight.

But Furlie had never been in a fight in all his life.

The truth is *Furlie was a fraidy cat.*

Blue jays scared Furlie.

Sounds scared Furlie.

He was even scared by his own shadow.

And when Oscar the dog next door barked, Furlie ran inside and hid.

That's why Furlie spent most of the day indoors, sitting on the windowsill and looking out at the world.

Here he was safe. Safe from the blue jays who squawked at him. Safe from the chittering squirrels who scolded him.

And safe from Oscar, the barking dog.

Yes, Furlie was safe sitting on the windowsill looking out—but he wasn't happy.

He saw the yellow marigolds blooming beside the wooden gate, and the bright butterflies skipping from flower to flower.

He saw the green leaves unfold on the crooked climbing tree, and the squirrels jumping from limb to limb.

Furlie didn't want to be a dull indoor cat. He wanted to be an exciting, outdoor cat.

He wanted to play in the marigolds

...and chase after the butterflies

...and climb the crooked tree.

Maybe, if he practiced being brave, he wouldn't be so afraid.

So every day, Furlie practiced being brave.

He practiced fierce faces in the mirror.

He practiced on his shadow.

He even practiced his growls
on the mouse in the attic.
It did seem to help.
Every day Furlie felt a little braver.

One morning, after lapping up his usual breakfast of a saucer of milk and fish tidbits, Furlie felt brave enough to go outside.

Oscar the dog next door was taking his morning nap. Furlie decided to practice being brave. He sneaked close. He arched his back and made his hair stand on end.

Furlie forgot that he was practicing on a *real* dog.

With a terrifying screech, he leaped straight at Oscar.

"HISSsstt!

MEOWWww!"

Poor Oscar almost jumped out of his fur!

For the first time in his life
Furlie had scared something,
instead of something scaring him.

He felt good.

He felt *power*.

He felt like a *real TIGER*!

He saw a bunch of leaves and jumped at them. "MRROW!" He hissed and spit, slapping the leaves into the air.

He pranced around the yard singing.

"I'M the biggest, strongest
CAT in all the jungle.
When the animals hear me rumble
They all run and squeak and stumble
'Cause I'm no Fraidy Cat!"

The song made Furlie feel really brave—so brave that he scared all the birds away from the birdbath.

From that day on, every morning after his breakfast, he went outside and found someone to scare.

Furlie Cat became the biggest bully in the neighborhood. He strolled down the street, holding his head high and his tail straight up.

No longer was he "Fraidycat Furlie."

Now he was "Fearless Furlie."

And "Fierce Furlie."

And sometimes, even

"FEROCIOUS
FURLIE!"

"I'M the biggest, strongest
CAT in all the jungle.
When the animals hear me rumble
They all run and squeak and stumble
'Cause I'm no Fraidy Cat!"

Suddenly, just ahead, he saw two furry round ears sticking up from a bush. His tail switching with excitement, Furlie crouched and then he pounced!

"HISSsstt!

MEOWWwww!"

A young bear cub sat in the bush eating blueberries. He was so surprised to see the hissing, yowling cat that he stood high on his hind legs. He growled, pretending to be brave.

"GRRRrrr!"

Poor Furlie! He'd never seen such a scary creature. Every hair on his back raised up. Furlie was so afraid that he couldn't even move a whisker.

The curious young bear took a step toward him.

Furlie let out a screech and ran to the nearest tree, climbing to the very top.

The young bear came close and looked up at Furlie. Now that the hissing creature was high in the tree, the bear cub felt more comfortable. He turned and rubbed his back hard against the tree trunk, scratching an itch. Then he ambled away to eat his breakfast in a quieter place.

Furlie clung to his tree limb, shivering.

That night, when the moon came out
he heard strange and scary sounds
...the hunting call of a screech owl
...the stealthy padded movements
of night hunters below.
For the first time Furlie felt
what it was like to be in real danger.

As he crouched on the tree branch, Furlie thought of the animals he had frightened. They must have been as afraid of him as he was now. He felt ashamed.

If he ever got back home safe, he knew that he'd never, NEVER bully anyone again.

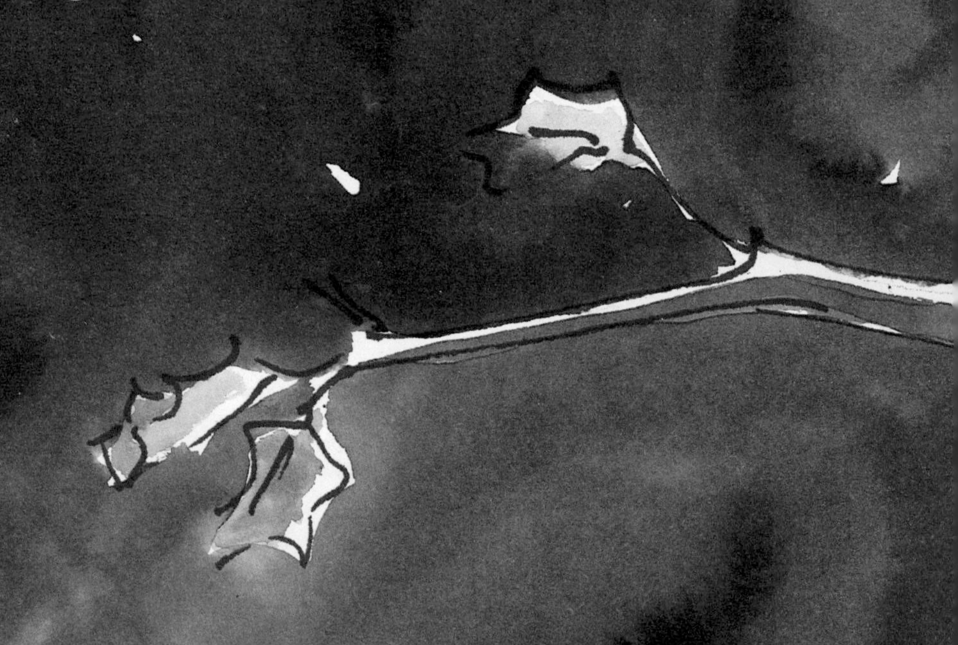

No longer was he the
biggest, strongest,
cat in all the jungle.

Now he was only a small orange
house cat, cold, and hungry, and *alone*.
All night he stayed high in the tree.

Early the next morning Furlie heard a familiar bark. It sounded like Oscar the dog next door.

"Woof!"

It was Oscar, woofing and wagging his tail, as though saying, "Come down. It's safe now."

Slowly and carefully,
Furlie backed down the tree.

Then jumping over the grasses,
he followed Oscar home.

From that day Oscar and Furlie became the best of friends.

Sometimes Furlie Cat still feels afraid, but now he doesn't always run away to hide. He sings his song, but very quietly—

and only

to himself.